P9-DMS-972

THE ADVENTURES OF

THE KNIGHTS' TALES

THE ADVENTURES OF

Sir Balin the Ill-Fated

GERALD MORRIS

⟶ ILLUSTRATED BY ⟵

AARON RENIER

tHoughton Mifflin Books for Children
Houghton Mifflin Harcourt
Boston New York 2012

Houghton Mifflin Books for Children is an imprint of
Houghton Mifflin Harcourt Publishing Company.

www.hmhbooks.com

The text of this book is set in Post Mediaeval.
The illustrations are brush and ink.

Library of Congress Cataloging-in-Publication Data
Morris, Gerald, 1963–.
The adventures of Sir Balin the Ill-fated / by Gerald Morris ; illustrated by
Aaron Renier.
p. cm.
Summary: After receiving an ominous prophecy at his christening, Sir Balin lives
his life alternately trying to fulfill it and trying to avoid it.
ISBN 978-0-547-68085-9
[1. Knights and knighthood–Fiction. 2. Prophecies–Fiction. 3. Middle Ages–
Fiction.] I. Renier, Aaron, ill. II. Title.
PZ7.M82785Ab 2012
[Fic]–dc23
2011012238

Manufactured in the United States of America
DOC 10 9 8 7 6 5 4 3 2 1
4500344400

For my friends that came in pairs:

Mark and Mike,

Kurt and Tim,

Tim and Todd.

Contents

Prologue

On a quiet night in Northumberland, a family gathered in the richly furnished parlor of their castle. Beside a roaring fire stood a young father in a velvet robe. Nearby sat a young mother in the stylish gown of a noblewoman. A small boy slept on a rug by the fire, and an even smaller boy lay in a bassinet at his mother's feet.

"Well, I think it was a lovely christening," the
mother said contentedly.

The father smiled. "My dear, you would have
thought it was lovely if the sky had fallen during
the service. Remember how it stormed the night
that Balan was christened? You said that was
lovely, too."

"It was," the mother replied. She looked at the baby in the basket. "Isn't he beautiful?"

The father smiled again. "My dear, you would say he was beautiful even if—"

"I *said*, 'Isn't he beautiful?'" interrupted the mother.

"Yes, dear. Very beautiful."

At that moment, the parlor door burst open. The fire shuddered in a cold draft, and a gray woman in a gray cloak tapped into the room, supported by a curiously carved staff.

The man stepped between the stranger and his wife. "I say, who the deuce are you?"

"I," said the woman, pausing dramatically, "I am . . . the Old Woman of the Mountain!"

"Which mountain?" asked the father.

"It matters not," replied the Old Woman of the Mountain, waving her hand dismissively.

The father frowned. "It matters when you're trying to get home, doesn't it? I mean, deuce it, how do you know when you've arrived if it isn't a particular—?"

"Hush!" intoned the Old Woman of a Mountain. "I am here for your son's christening!"

"That's so kind of you," said the mother. "But, you know, the service ended more than an hour ago."

"What? Isn't it at four o'clock?"

"Yes, it was," said the father and mother together. The Old Woman of a Mountain Somewhere scowled, and the mother added, "I'm sure it's not your fault. The days are getting shorter all the time, and it's easy to get confused."

"Hang on," said the father, "let me think about that. If she was confused by the days getting shorter, wouldn't she have been an hour early?"

"No, dear," said the mother. "If she thought it was three because of the daylight—"

"Hush!" repeated the Old Woman of Some Mountain. "I am here for your son's sake! I will tell you his future and his blessing!"

"Isn't that lovely?" beamed the mother. "Will he marry a nice northern girl?"

"Why do you want to do that?" the father asked the gray woman.

"It is what the Old Woman of the Mountain does!" she explained.

"You didn't do it when our older son, Balan, was christened," the father pointed out.

The old woman reddened slightly. "I *meant* to," she said. "But it was raining that day. I thought it might clear up, so I waited, but it never did."

"How can you tell my son's future if you can't even tell if it's going to stop raining?" asked the father.

"I do babies, not weather," said the old woman. "What is your child's name?"

The mother tickled her infant's chin and said, "This is Balin."

The old woman opened her mouth, then hesitated. "But isn't that your older son's name?"

"No, no," the mother explained. "My older son is Balan."

"Eh?"

"Ba*lin* and Ba*lan*," the mother enunciated.

"Won't that be a problem?" asked the old

woman. "I mean, really! Matching names?" She looked at the father, who peeked at his wife from the corner of his eye, then shrugged.

The mother smiled dreamily. "My boys will match in every way. They'll wear matching clothes and have matching coverlets on their beds and matching curtains on their windows and be the very best of friends."

The Old Woman of a Mountain looked faintly ill. "You're joking, right?"

"No, why?"

The crone looked again at the father. "They'll hate it. You know that, don't you? I mean, seriously, you can't let—"

The father avoided his wife's eyes and cleared his throat. "Look here, weren't you going to bless Balin or something?"

"Very well," she said, with a shrug. Tapping her way over, she held her hand above the infant.

"Ah!" she said. The young parents waited expectantly, but for a long minute she said nothing more.

"Is, um, is that it?" asked the father at last.

The old woman ignored him. "I see greatness in this child!" she said at last. The mother smiled. "He shall be known as the noblest knight in England! But wait! There's more. I see a cloud over his greatness! Like the mist on the mountain!"

"Which mountain?" asked the father.

"And will he marry a nice northern girl?" asked the mother.

"I see destruction and calamity! His greatness shall bring misfortune on all his companions! He shall do marvelous deeds, but they will only serve him ill! In one day, he shall bring down two kingdoms! He shall strike the Dolorous Stroke!"

"The *what* stroke?" asked the father.

"The dolorous one." The father frowned, and the old woman added, "It means 'sad.'"

"Why not say 'sad,' then?" asked the father.

"He shall be brave above all knights! He shall never refuse an adventure!"

"That's nice," the mother said. "Now, when he gets married—"

"But all his adventures shall bring misfortune!"

The father stepped forward and took the old woman's elbow. "Well, I want to thank you for stopping by. It's been—"

"And in the end," the old woman said, "he shall destroy the knight whom he loves most in the world!"

A deathly silence hung over the parlor. The Old Woman of an Unknown Mountain wrapped her gray cloak about her defiantly. At last the child's father said, "Look here, if that's the best blessing you have to offer, I'm *glad* you missed Balan's christening. Now, if you're done, I don't want to keep you."

"I have spoken!" the old woman declared.

"Yes, we heard you," said the father, ushering her to the door. "And to be perfectly frank, we all wish you'd put a cork in it instead." He guided her out the door, then closed it firmly behind her.

"Never mind, dear," said the mother, tickling her infant's chin again. "*I* know you'll marry a nice northern girl."

The father looked at his son thoughtfully. "You sure have an awful lot of destiny hanging over you, little snip," he murmured.

"He's *not* a little snip!" the mother declared stoutly.

"No, dear, of course not," said the father, but still he looked grave.

CHAPTER 1
The Knight with Two Swords

On a day some twenty years after these events, King Arthur held court. Now, most people know that King Arthur became king by drawing an enchanted sword from a stone. Many also know that he established a band of noble heroes called the Knights of the Round Table. Some even know that he ruled wisely and well and brought peace to all England. But not many realize how long all this took. On this particular day, the king had already drawn the sword from the stone, but he had no Round Table and only a few knights, and he ruled only a small part of England. Many powerful nobles were waging war with him, resisting his reign, which kept King Arthur quite busy. Nevertheless, he was already trying to rule wisely and well, which was why he was holding court. He was hearing the appeals of the people and administering justice.

"Next case!" called Sir Kay, the king's foster brother, who stood beside the throne, sorting out the crowd and keeping order. Two guards led forward a grimy knight in dusty armor. Sir Kay looked at his list. "Here, O king, we have a knight who is accused of killing a fellow knight, a certain—" Sir Kay paused, squinting at the records in front of him. "Oh, dear."

"What is it, Kay?" asked the king.

"He's accused of killing our cousin, Sir Bullevere. Uncle Clovis's son."

King Arthur said, "This is a serious charge, O
knight." He looked disapprovingly at the knight's

dusty armor. "Though you don't seem to take it seriously. Is this how you choose to appear before your king?"

The knight replied softly, "I did not choose this dirt, sire. I have spent the last three months in your dungeons, waiting for trial. Your dungeons could use a wash."

The king's expression softened. "I see. I'm afraid it *has* been a while since I last held court, hasn't it? You see, I've been busy lately, fighting the rebel King Royns of Wales. Well, never mind the dust, then. What is your name?"

"I am Sir Balin of Northumberland, Your Highness," said the knight.

"Sir Balin, you are accused of killing the knight Sir Bullevere."

"Yes, I did that."

King Arthur blinked. "You admit it?" Sir Balin nodded. "Why did you do it?"

"He attacked me."

"Unprovoked?"

"No, sire. I think he attacked me because I called him a nasty, cowardly brute."

King Arthur frowned again. "To provoke another to attack is the same as attacking yourself," he said.

Beside the king, Sir Kay cleared his throat. "Um, Arthur?"

"Yes, Kay?"

"I'd just like to point out that, in fact, Bullevere *was* a nasty, cowardly brute. I mean, remember that Christmas we spent at Uncle Clovis's? Bull was a stinker, all right."

"But you can't just go around calling people names," the king said.

"Even if they're true?" asked Sir Kay. "Why not?"

"Because it starts fights, and people get killed," King Arthur explained patiently. "Sir Balin, step forward to receive your sentence."

But before Sir Balin could move, a murmur arose from the onlookers. The crowd parted to make way for a tall woman, who strode forward wearing a long sword.

"Where is King Arthur?" demanded the woman austerely.

No one spoke. Since King Arthur was wearing a crown and sitting on a throne in the middle of the hall, this seemed rather obvious, and people hate answering silly questions. But the woman apparently expected an answer, so at last the king waved his hand and said, "Um, right here."

"At last! Long have I sought you!"

There was another pause. "Well, ah . . . here I am."

"I am Lady Lyla of the Outer Isles! I bring this enchanted sword, seeking the one knight who is able to draw it from its sheath!"

"Stuck, is it?" asked Sir Kay.

"I used to have a sword that would do that," said another knight. "Have you tried jiggling the hilt?"

"No, you need to tap it on the side," said another.

"Bacon grease," added a third. "That's the best way to—"

"It is *not* stuck!" said the woman. "It is enchanted! Only the noblest knight in England may draw this blade, and for that knight it will come forth easily."

"Oh!" said all the king's knights.

"It's like your sword, Excalibur," Sir Kay said to the king. "No one but you could draw it from the stone. You'd better take this, sire."

"Very well," said King Arthur. He rose from his throne and went to Lady Lyla. She held the scabbard firmly in both hands as the king grasped the sword's hilt and pulled. The sword didn't move. The king frowned and tugged again, with the same result.

"Pulling harder will avail you nothing," declared Lady Lyla. "Only the noblest knight in England may draw this blade, and for that knight it will come forth easily."

"Yes, you mentioned that," muttered the king. "Give it a go, Kay?"

One by one, all Arthur's knights tried the sword, but none could budge it by a hair. "Alas!" cried Lady Lyla. "Where shall I find the noblest knight in England?"

Suddenly a strange knight stepped from the crowd. "Let me try!" he said.

"Who are you, O knight?" asked Lady Lyla.

"I am Sir Lanceor of Ireland. I have come to join King Arthur and to prove myself to him! May I attempt the adventure of the enchanted blade?"

Lady Lyla released the sword's sheath, letting it hang loosely by her side. "Any knight may try," she said.

Sir Lanceor struck a dramatic pose, lifted his chin, and said, "I know not whether I am the noblest knight in England, but I am willing to put myself to the test. Shall I, peradventure, succeed where so many noble knights have essayed this trial and . . . ?"

While Sir Lanceor was delivering this speech, the dusty knight Sir Balin stepped up behind Lady Lyla and easily drew the sword from its scabbard. Everyone stared, except for Sir Lanceor, who was too busy talking. " . . . t'would be a marvel indeed for an unknown knight to step so quickly to so high a rank, but—"

"What do you think you're doing?" demanded Lady Lyla to Sir Balin. Her face was alarmingly purple.

"Drawing the enchanted sword," Sir Balin explained. "You see, when I was born, the Old Woman of the Mountain prophesied that one day I would be the noblest knight in England, so when you said—"

"I don't care what some old wench said to you," snarled Lady Lyla. "Give it back!"

"No," said Sir Balin. "It's mine now. I drew it. King Arthur got to keep Excalibur when he drew it from the stone, didn't he?"

"That's true," said Sir Kay.

"Give it to me!" Lady Lyla shrieked. "If you don't return it at once, terrible misfortune will follow you wherever you go!"

Sir Balin shrugged. "Yes, I know. Can I have the scabbard, too?"

With a scream of fury, Lady Lyla threw herself at Sir Balin, but as it happened, Sir Balin had just lowered the sword to examine an odd notch in the blade near the hilt, and Lady Lyla threw herself right onto the point. It pierced her heart, and she fell dead at Sir Balin's feet.

"Oh, dear," said Sir Balin. He glanced at the king. "That was an accident, sire."

"I know," said the king. "I was watching. Bad luck for her, though."

Sir Balin sighed. "It's that prophecy again."

"What prophecy?" asked the king.

"The same one that said I would be known as the noblest knight in England," Sir Balin said. "It also said I would bring misfortune everywhere I went. It's true. Things always go badly for me. It's like when I met your cousin Sir Bullevere. He was beating a peasant with a switch for not getting out of his way, and I only meant to stop him from being such a beast, but then he attacked and I ended up killing him

and spending the whole summer in your dungeons. Things always go sour around me."

"I see," said the king.

"So, unless you want to throw me back in your dungeons—"

"I don't," said the king.

"—then probably the best thing I could do for your court is get far away so none of my ill luck rubs off on you. May I?"

"You may do whatever you wish, Sir Balin. You are free."

"Free? Hardly," muttered Sir Balin. Stooping, he took the scabbard from Lady Lyla's body.

"Here, don't I get a try, too?" asked a plaintive voice. It was Sir Lanceor.

King Arthur raised one eyebrow. "Why? Lady Lyla said only one knight could do it, and one knight has done it."

Sir Lanceor started to speak, then clamped his lips shut and stomped away.

Sir Balin turned to leave, but Sir Kay said, "Just a moment, Sir Balin. It says in the records that you had a horse and a sword when you were arrested. I've sent for them."

"Thank you," said Sir Balin.

"I guess you have two swords now," said Sir Kay.

Sir Balin sighed heavily. "I'll probably need them."

CHAPTER 2
The Knight He Loves
Most in the World

Sir Balin rode alone through the forest, reflecting glumly on his fate: a knight destined by an old prophecy to ride alone forever or bring disaster on his companions. If you said it right, it sounded very adventurous and romantic, but in practice it wasn't so exciting. It was just lonely.

He wasn't alone for long, though. Only half an

hour from King Arthur's court, a knight rode out of the forest and pointed a lance at him. "There you are, you curst marplot!" exclaimed the knight.

"Curst *what?*" asked Sir Balin. "And who are you, anyway? Do I know you?" The knight's visor was down, hiding his face.

"I am Sir Lanceor of Ireland, and I called you a *marplot!* Someone who ruins everything!"

Sir Balin nodded. "That's me, I'm afraid. It's my fate."

"Well, you shall meet a worse fate now!" Sir Lanceor shouted. Spurring his horse forward, he aimed his lance at Sir Balin's breastplate.

Now, some might consider this a very unsporting action, inasmuch as Sir Balin wasn't carrying a lance himself, but it worked out all right. It actually isn't that difficult to dodge a lance aimed by a galloping knight. Sir Balin simply leaned to one side, making the point miss, which meant that Sir

Lanceor couldn't do anything until he had stopped his horse and turned around, which took several seconds. (Really, people should have noticed early on how inefficient fighting with a lance actually is, but oddly enough, it never seemed to sink in. People kept on pointing lances at each other, and mostly missing, for years and years.)

Sir Balin drew both his swords and rode after Sir Lanceor. With one sword he knocked the lance from the knight's grasp and with the other bashed him from his horse. Sir Lanceor landed with a thump, then lay still. Sir Balin dismounted and stood over Sir Lanceor's inert figure. Still no movement. Cautiously, he checked the knight. Sir Lanceor was out cold. He must have fallen on his head. Sir Balin took Sir Lanceor's lance and broke it in pieces, then threw Sir Lanceor's sword up in the topmost branches of an oak, then mounted his horse to ride away. Only then did he notice that

he was being watched by an old man in flowing black robes.

"Who are you?" asked Sir Balin.

"I . . . I am . . . the Old Man of the Meadow."

Sir Balin suppressed the impulse to ask which meadow. Instead he said, "Please don't tell me that you're an enchanter."

"I am! And I have been watching you! You defeated that knight easily!"

"It was just luck," Sir Balin said. "His bad luck, I mean. He fell badly."

"It was not luck!" declared the Old Man of Some Meadow. "It was fate! You bear the aura of prophecy about you! What is your name, O Knight of Destiny?"

"I'm . . . uh . . . just call me the Knight with Two Swords."

"O Knight with Two Swords, I see . . . yes, I see a great destiny for you!"

"I know, I know," Sir Balin said wearily. "I shall be the noblest knight in England and shall never refuse an adventure and bring down two kingdoms in one day, but everything will go bad for me, and I'll bring misfortune on all my companions and strike the Something-that-starts-with-a-D Stroke and in the end shall destroy the knight I love most in the world. So you see, I'm already full to the brim with prophetic destiny and don't have room for even a little bit more. Good day." Sir Balin rode away, leaving the Old Man of the Meadow to do whatever enchanters did when they were alone.

Soon Sir Balin came upon another knight traveling through the forest. Both knights lowered their visors, gripped their swords, and slowed their horses. When they were twenty yards away, the two knights stopped. They looked at each other through their helmets for a long time.

"Are you going to attack me?" asked Sir Balin.

"Why would I want to do that?" the strange knight replied.

"I'm sure I don't know, but knights are always doing it anyway. There was Sir Bullevere and then Sir Lanceor, and I didn't want to fight either of them, but I killed the first and knocked the other one out."

"You sound like you're bragging," said the strange knight.

"Bragging!" exclaimed Sir Balin, annoyed. "Why would I brag about bringing misfortune on everyone I meet! It's a curse, not an achievement! I can't help it! When I was christened, I was laid under a horrible fate that I would be the noblest—"

"Oh, put a cork in it," said the strange knight. "Are you still obsessed with that silly prophecy nonsense? How many times do I have to tell you it's all rot?"

"Eh?" said Sir Balin. He raised his visor to reveal a growing smile.

The strange knight raised his to show a matching smile. "Having a bad day, little brother?" he asked.

The two knights rode together and embraced joyfully. "Lannie!" Sir Balin shouted, for of course the Old Woman of a Mountain had been right that the names Balin and Balan were too similar. The brothers had gotten confused from the beginning, so that soon they had become Lannie and Lin to everyone except their mother.

"Here now, none that 'Lannie' business," exclaimed Sir Balan. "I'm Sir Balan the Doughty now."

"The what?"

"Doughty. D-O-U-G-H-T-Y. They tell me it means courageous."

"I see," said Sir Balin politely. "Yes, of course. Very likely."

"Put a cork in it, Lin," Sir Balan chuckled. "I didn't choose the name. I just came through a couple of adventures, and people started calling me by it. And where the deuce have you been? You missed Mother's birthday last month."

"Cripes!" Sir Balin said, slapping his heavy metal gauntlet against his helmet with a clang. "I forgot all about it! But it's not my fault; I was in prison."

"Hmm," Sir Balan said. "Maybe you'd better come up with a different excuse to give her. Just a thought. What were you doing in prison?"

"It's a long story," Sir Balin sighed.

"Then hadn't we ought to make camp and hear it?" replied Sir Balan with a smile.

So the brothers made camp, and Sir Balin recounted all that had happened to him. When he got to the part about Lady Lyla and the enchanted sword, Sir Balan said, "I wondered why you were carrying a spare. May I see the enchanted sword?"

Sir Balin handed the sword and scabbard to his brother. "Sure," he said, "but you won't be able to pull it out, because only the—"

Sir Balan pulled the sword easily from the scabbard.

"Eh?" said Sir Balin. "But only the noblest knight in England could do that, and everybody else tried and failed, but I knew I would succeed because of the prophecy from the Old Woman of—"

"Apparently I'm also the noblest knight in England," Sir Balan said. "Even without a prophecy." He peered closely at the scabbard. "I say, when everyone tried to pull it out and failed, was Lady Lyla holding it like this?" He held it firmly by the scabbard.

Sir Balin nodded. "Yes, just like that."

"Try it, little brother," Sir Balan said. Sir Balin grasped the hilt and pulled, but it didn't move. Sir Balan chuckled. "There's a secret catch in the scabbard here," he said, pointing. "If you hold it down, it fits into that little notch in the blade and locks it in place. If you let go, the sword comes out easily."

Sir Balin examined the secret lock in the scabbard for a minute. "So it was all a trick?" he said at last.

Sir Balan nodded. "I'd guess that Lady Lyla and your Sir Lanceor were working together. She would hold the sword locked while everyone else tried, then release it for him. He would draw the sword and be known right away as the noblest knight in England."

"That's why Lady Lyla was so angry when I

drew it out," Sir Balin mused. "And why Sir Lanceor followed me and attacked me later. Because I had ruined their plan."

"Very good!" Sir Balan said, grinning. "You're not so dumb. I don't care what everyone says."

Sir Balin ignored him. "So it wasn't an enchantment; it was just a made-up story."

"They're all made-up stories," Sir Balan said. "I keep telling you that. So is the Old Mountain Wench's prophecy. It's all blather."

Sir Balin shook his head slowly. "No, she was right. According to Father, the prophecy was that I would be *known* as the noblest knight in England. Well, since I drew this sword, all the king's court knows me as the noblest knight in England. Lady Lyla might have been pitching a lie, but the Old Woman of a Mountain told the truth. Besides, the rest of her prophecy is also proving true."

"You mean you've overthrown two kingdoms in one day and struck the Dubious Stroke?"

"No, not those bits yet. And it's not Dubious; it's some other D word. But the rest of the prophecy is true: every great thing I do turns sour and goes badly. Ill fortune follows me everywhere." Sir Balan rolled his eyes, but he said nothing. Sir Balin continued, "That's why I left King Arthur's court. He's the rightful king of England, and I don't want any of my wretched fate to rub off on him. He has enough trouble."

"That much is true, anyway," agreed Sir Balan. "Why, just three miles from here, King Royns of Wales is setting up for an attack on Arthur. I almost ran into them a couple of hours ago. What is it, Lin?"

"That's it!" Sir Balin crowed. "That's what I can do to help King Arthur! I can't stay with him because of the ill fortune that follows me, but I can go bring my bad luck on King Royns!"

"I beg your pardon?" asked Sir Balan.

"I'll go join King Royns and let my curse do

the rest. He'll be begging for mercy in a week!"

"You're daft, Lin," Sir Balan said. "I mean that. You've really gone off the edge this time. Listen to my words: *There is no curse!*"

But Sir Balin was already climbing back on his horse. "You'll see, when things start going wrong for King Royns." Sir Balan sighed, but he climbed on his horse as well. "Oh, are you coming with me?" asked Sir Balin.

"Mother would never forgive me if I let you wander alone in your feeble-minded state," retorted his brother.

A quarter of an hour later, the two brothers rode out of the forest onto a grassy plain, where a lone knight in gilded armor sat on a horse, watching them approach. "There you are at last!" the glittering knight said.

Sir Balin and Sir Balan looked at each other. Sir Balan said, "Yes, here we are." It was true, after all.

"Which one of you is Lanceor?" the gilded

knight asked. The brothers looked at each other again, but before either could answer, the knight went on, "Never mind. I don't care. I don't need to know the names of my spies. You're late, you know. What news do you have from King Arthur's camp? Are they expecting us?"

"Um, before we give our report," Sir Balin said, "you need to identify yourself."

"King Royns of Wales, of course! Who else do you think would have armor like this? By my father's beard, if I had known you were idiots I would never have hired you as spies. But your letter said you had a foolproof way to get into Arthur's inner circle. Now give me your report. Are we going to have a surprise or not?"

The brothers looked at each other, then drew their swords—all three of them—and placed the points at King Royns's neck. "Surprise," said Sir Balan.

Two hours later, Sir Balin and Sir Balan dropped a securely bound King Royns of Wales at the feet of King Arthur. "We thought it would be best for you to take charge of this gentleman," Sir Balin said. "King Royns will do less harm in your hands, I think."

King Arthur and all his knights stared at the prisoner in astonishment. "King Royns?" the king repeated. "But I thought you were still in Glouce-ster."

"That's what you were supposed to think," King Royns growled. "My army's just a few miles away, and we would have taken you completely unaware if these two knights hadn't stumbled on me. I had a perfect battle plan, and it's all gone sour now, out of just pure bad luck."

"Bad luck's my specialty," Sir Balin said modestly.

"Sir Balin," King Arthur said, "we are in your debt. You may have saved the kingdom today. Will you introduce me to your companion?"

"Of course, sire," said Sir Balin. "This is my brother, Sir Balan the Doughy."

"Not *doughy*, you ninny," hissed Sir Balan. *"Doughty."*

Sir Balin grinned merrily. "My mistake. Doughty. Of course. Let me try again. King Arthur, this is Sir Balan, the knight I love most in the world."

Then Sir Balin's eyes widened, and his smile froze.

CHAPTER 3

The Questing Lady

Sir Balin rode alone over the dales. He had to. As soon as he had realized that his brother was the knight he loved most in the world, he had realized he had to stay as far away from him as possible.

Of course, Sir Balan had not seen it that way. "You cloth-headed bungle-noggin!" Sir Balan had exclaimed wrathfully. "When will you stop letting that silly prophecy run your life?"

"But I don't *want* to destroy you," Sir Balin had explained.

"Then here's an idea," Sir Balan had retorted. "Don't."

"It's not that simple!"

"It's exactly that simple!"

"I can't risk it," Sir Balin said pleadingly. "I might kill you by accident or something."

Sir Balan snorted and said, "Fine!"

"I just want you to understand," Sir Balin said.

"Oh, put a cork in it," snapped Sir Balan, and that was how the brothers had parted ways and how Sir Balin happened to be alone when he came upon a lady, standing beside a tall tree, staring up into its branches. Two horses grazed nearby.

"Oh, for heaven's sake, come down," the lady was saying.

"Is it a knight?" came a muffled voice from the tree.

"Of course it's a knight."

"Describe him," said the voice.

"Just a normal knight. Ordinary gray armor. No shield, but two swords. Hmm, that's interesting."

The tree's foliage rustled, and a knight dropped from the branches. He peered at Sir Balin, then said, "Whew!"

"Look here," the lady began, "are you going to climb a tree or jump into the bushes every time we meet anyone? Because if so, we'll never get anywhere."

"You don't understand," said the knight.

"Try me," replied the lady.

"Even if I told you, you wouldn't believe me," the knight said.

By this time, Sir Balin had joined them. "Good afternoon," he said.

"Good afternoon, Sir Knight," the lady replied.

"I'm Sir Balin, the Knight with Two Swords," Sir Balin said. He had decided to stick with that nickname.

"Good thing you have two swords, then," the lady replied promptly. "Because if you only had one, your name would sound silly."

Sir Balin grinned. "Or if I had three."

The lady returned his smile. "Very true. What a stroke of luck that you have exactly the right number of swords for your name. I'm Lady Annalise, the Questing Lady."

"The *what?*" asked Sir Balin. "What's a questing lady?"

"A lady who accompanies knights on quests, of course."

"I see," said Sir Balin. "That makes sense, I suppose. Have you, er, been doing this for long?"

"Oh, yes," said Lady Annalise. "Years and years. It's a family tradition. My mother was a Questing Lady before me, and I'm carrying on the family trade." Then Lady Annalise's brow darkened, and she muttered, "*Somebody* has to, anyway."

Sir Balin raised one eyebrow questioningly, and Lady Annalise said, "Sorry. I was thinking of my younger sister, who would have made a great Questing Lady, but no, she couldn't be bothered with the family heritage. She's off at school now, studying to be a Damsel in Distress, if you can imagine! A simpering, moaning, pathetic *Damsel in Distress!* Nearly broke Mother's heart."

Sir Balin tried to think of something sympathetic to say. "Young people today," he murmured. "No respect for tradition."

"Exactly!" agreed Lady Annalise.

"And, er, are you on a quest right now?" asked Sir Balin.

Lady Annalise gave a sidelong glance at her companion, who had climbed back on his horse but still looked nervous. "Not really," she said. "I was between quests—it's the slow season just now—and I met Sir Harleus Le Berbeus here and thought he might do. But it turns out he mostly quests for good hiding places."

At this, Sir Harleus Le Berbeus spoke. "You'd hide, too, if you were faced with the danger that I'm faced with."

"What danger is that?" asked Sir Balin.

"You wouldn't believe me if I told you."

"That's all I can get out of him, too," said Lady Annalise. "Some danger he won't name."

"Oh, I can name it," said Sir Harleus Le Berbeus. "Its name is Sir Gorlon."

"That's it? One knight?" demanded Lady Annalise. "What's so terrible about this Sir Gorlon?"

"You wouldn't believe me if I told you."

Lady Annalise shook her head disgustedly, and Sir Balin suppressed a smile. "Well, Sir Harleus Le Berbeus, if there's anything I can do—"

"Seriously?" demanded Sir Harleus Le Berbeus. "You'll help? Will you ride with me and protect me?"

"Well, I'm not sure if my presence will be more protection or—"

"I accept your offer!" exclaimed Sir Harleus Le Berbeus. "Promise me that you won't desert me. Promise me that you'll protect me from Sir Gorlon!"

"Well, sure, I'll do what I can, but what I'm trying to say is—"

He never finished his sentence. There was a sudden drumming of hoofbeats, coming from nowhere, and Sir Harleus Le Berbeus flew from his saddle and landed on the ground. He gasped and coughed. Lady Annalise threw herself from her saddle and ran to him. For several moments she worked over him, then rose to her feet. Sir Harleus Le Berbeus was still.

"Is he dead?" asked Sir Balin.

"No, but he's badly hurt. He needs a doctor. Fortunately, I know a monastery a few miles away where he can be cared for."

"What happened?"

Lady Annalise hesitated, then said, "Before he passed out, he said it was Sir Gorlon."

"Sir Gorlon? But there wasn't anyone—"

"Sir Gorlon the Invisible Knight."

Sir Balin and Lady Annalise transported Sir Harleus Le Berbeus to the monastery, then rode away together. When they had gone about a mile, Lady Annalise cocked her head and looked at Sir

Balin. "I say, I don't suppose you're on a quest," she said. "Because, strictly speaking, I'm only supposed to ride with questing knights."

Sir Balin pondered this for a moment, then said, "Well, I wasn't a couple of hours ago, but I am now."

"Oh?"

"I want to find this Sir Gorlon," Sir Balin said. "It's not right to go around attacking people without warning. Besides, I told Sir Harleus Le Berbeus I'd protect him, then I didn't, and it makes me angry."

Lady Annalise nodded approvingly. "An excellent quest," she said.

They rode together for another hour, chatting in perfect accord and enjoying each other's company very much indeed, until they came to a small hut in a forest, where a brown-robed hermit was talking with a young knight.

"Hello," Sir Balin called out.

"Good evening," replied the hermit.

"Wotcher!" said the young knight.

"Er, what was that?" asked Sir Balin.

"It means 'What ho!' don't you know. 'Pip pip!'"

"I see," said Sir Balin.

"My name is Sir Peryn de Monte Belyard," the young knight said.

"I'm Sir Balin, the Knight with Two Swords, and this is Lady Annalise, the Questing Lady."

Sir Peryn's mouth dropped open. "An actual Questing Lady? Really? I'm honored to meet you, ma'am. My father traveled with a Questing Lady once, a Lady Brigitta."

"My mother," said Lady Annalise, smiling.

"Are you on a quest now?" asked Sir Peryn de Monte Belyard. "May I join you?"

Lady Annalise bowed slightly. "I'll have to ask Sir Balin here, of course, but—"

"Down!" shouted Sir Balin abruptly. He had just heard the sound of drumming hoofbeats. He threw himself to one side, knocking Lady Annalise from her saddle to the ground. There was a sharp cry of pain, and then the hoofbeats faded away into the forest.

Sir Balin checked Lady Annalise first. "Are you hurt?"

"I'm fine," she said. "Thank you. Go to Sir Peryn."

They both rushed to where Sir Peryn lay on the ground, clutching his arm, which was welling blood.

"Curse you, Sir Gorlon," shouted the hermit suddenly. "If I weren't a man of peace, I'd take a sword and—"

"Don't worry," Sir Balin said. "I'll take care of Sir Gorlon. That's my quest. Can you help us with Sir Peryn?"

Together the three made Sir Peryn de Monte Belyard comfortable on a pallet in the hermitage.

He wasn't badly hurt, but soon went to sleep from the shock and loss of blood. The hermit led them outside.

"Are you really after Sir Gorlon?"

"I am," Sir Balin said. "Although I don't have any idea how to look for an invisible knight."

"I can help then," the holy man said. "He isn't always invisible. When he's at home and feels safe, he lets himself be seen."

"Where is his home?"

"He lives with his brother, who calls himself King Perleus. Perleus's castle is just between those two hills to the east. Its towers are high, its moat is wide, and it's guarded by a hundred armed knights. But if you want to defeat Sir Gorlon, it will have to be there."

Sir Balin glanced at Lady Annalise and smiled. "Coming?" he said.

"Of course I'm coming. It's what I do."

Chapter 4
The Dolorous Stroke

As it was already late, Sir Balin and Lady Annalise stopped after only an hour to make camp. Sir Balin was struck again by how pleasant a companion Lady Annalise was. Her conversation was witty and thoughtful, but she didn't feel the need to talk all the time, either. As they tended their tired horses, Sir Balin said, "I've never quested with a Questing Lady before, but I have to say, it's an excellent way to quest. You make the time pass delightfully."

"Thank you, Sir Balin," Lady Annalise said demurely.

"Are all Questing Ladies as interesting as you?"

Lady Annalise hesitated, then said, "Actually, there's a bit of disagreement on that point within the Questing Ladies Guild."

"The what?"

"It's the organization that sets standards for the profession, trains apprentices, and all that. Anyway, some of the older Questing Ladies feel that our part is to cook and tidy up and speak only when spoken to." She sighed. "My grandmother was that type, and I can't help thinking she must have been a dead bore on the road."

"Rather!" Sir Balin agreed heartily. "You're not that type at all."

"No, I'm a companion, not a personal maid."

Sir Balin pursed his lips thoughtfully. "So, does that mean you don't, um . . . Well, as it happens, I'm a terrible cook."

"Me, too," Lady Annalise said promptly. "Sorry. My turn to ask you a question, though. Why do you wear two swords?"

"It started a week ago . . . Well, actually it started on my christening day. Do you mind a rather long story?" Lady Annalise begged him to continue, so Sir Balin told her about the Old Woman of a Mountain's prophecy, then explained to her the circumstances by which he had obtained the second sword from Lady Lyla. "So you see," he concluded, "when I drew the sword from the scabbard, I thought it was fate—the old prophecy coming true. Of course I had to keep the sword."

"But then your brother showed you the secret lock on the scabbard, so now you know it wasn't fate at all, just a muddled plot."

"Why shouldn't a muddled plot be a part of fate?"

Lady Annalise frowned. "I don't know, but it doesn't feel right. If *anything* that happens can be seen as the fulfillment of the prophecy, then the prophecy's not very useful, is it?"

"I've never thought the prophecy very useful," Sir Balin muttered. "Anyway, now that I've started calling myself the Knight with Two Swords, I sort of have to keep it around."

They arrived at King Perleus's castle around mid-morning the next day. The hermit had been right about the castle's defenses. The towers were high, the walls imposing, the moat wide, and the guards numerous.

"How are we ever going to get in there?" wondered Lady Annalise.

"Let's ask," said Sir Balin. He trotted up to the

nearest guard, who stood at the drawbridge. "Hello," he said to the guard.

"Move along," said the guard.

"But I'm here to visit King Perleus."

"My orders say that only unarmed people get in, no knights. Move along."

Lady Annalise asked, "What about unarmed knights?"

The guard looked confused. "All knights are armed. What would a knight be doing going about without weapons? Besides, you have a sword. I can see it."

"But what if Sir Balin gave you his sword? Then he would be unarmed."

Sir Balin realized that, from the way he was positioned on his horse, the guard could see only one of his swords. Slowly he lowered his arm to further conceal his second blade. The guard scratched his head. "I don't know. I never met a knight who'd give up his sword."

"Oh, I'll do it," Sir Balin said. He drew the sword that the guard could see from the scabbard and tossed it on the ground at the guard's feet. "Now can I go in? Your master did say to let unarmed people inside."

The guard shrugged. "Right, then. I think you're daft, but go ahead."

They trotted across the drawbridge, and as they entered the castle courtyard, Sir Balin said, "That was a brilliant thought, Lady Annalise."

"Thank you. Now be careful. Hide that second sword."

Sir Balin dismounted and took a blanket from his gear. With Lady Annalise's help, he draped it over his shoulder and tied it in place. It was awkward and bulky and hung around his ankles, but it did hide his second sword from view. "Shall we go look for Sir Gorlon?" Sir Balin said. "And hope we see him?"

They entered a large doorway and followed a

corridor until they came to a vast chamber with high ceilings. In the center of the room, on an ornate throne with two long axes crossed behind it, sat a man with a gray beard.

The man on the throne said nothing, but a stocky black-bearded man at his side growled, "Who are you?"

"I am Sir Balin, the Knight with . . . um . . . from Northumberland," Sir Balin said.

"How did you get past the gate?" demanded Stocky Black-Beard.

"The guard let me through once I handed over my sword," Sir Balin said. He showed them the empty scabbard at his side. "I am seeking Sir Gorlon, who is a coward and a villain, who attacks other knights while invisible."

Stocky Black-Beard grinned wolfishly and stepped forward. "I know you," he said. "You're the knight who jumped out of my way just in time yesterday and let me hit that young fellow instead. Have you come to punish me? Without a sword?"

"Then you're Sir Gorlon?" Sir Balin asked.

"That's *who* I am," sneered the knight. "But what you need to worry about is *where* I am." Sir Gorlon reached for his sword and was just beginning to draw the blade before he vanished completely from view.

Rapid footsteps approached and Sir Balin immediately stepped toward Lady Annalise and pushed her roughly away. "Get back!" he hissed. Something swished through the air by his head as Sir Gorlon struck at the spot where Sir Balin had just been standing. Sir Balin reached under his blanket to draw his second sword, but his hand got tangled up in the folds. Frantically he tugged the blanket away, but it was caught on the sword. He dropped to the ground and heard Sir Gorlon's second blow pass over his head.

With a final yank, Sir Balin managed to untangle the blanket and pull it off as he scrambled to his feet. "Ha!" he called. "I'm not unarmed after all!"

Grasping his scabbard firmly, he pulled at the sword. It didn't move.

"Blast!" he muttered. He threw himself backwards, barely evading a third blow from Sir Gorlon's invisible sword. He tugged again at his weapon, but it didn't move.

"Let go of the scabbard!" shouted Lady Annalise.

"Oh, right," said Sir Balin. He hadn't realized that he had the sword with the secret lock. Releasing the scabbard, he drew the blade out with a flourish. The sword came free, then stopped sharply in midair. Sir Balin tugged at it, but it was stuck. "Now what?" he muttered urgently.

Then, before his eyes, Sir Gorlon materialized— with Sir Balin's sword stuck in his heart. Sir Gorlon crumpled to the floor, and Sir Balin withdrew his weapon.

Slowly, the gray-bearded man rose to his feet. "Is he dead?" he asked.

Sir Balin nodded. "Are you King Perleus?"

"I am," replied the man. "Sir Balin, you have slain my wicked younger brother, he who has killed so many good knights and has enslaved so many good people and held my whole land in a reign of terror with his magical powers!"

Sir Balin blinked. This sounded promising. "Does that mean that you're not angry with me for killing your brother?"

King Perleus smiled, then said, "No, I'm wicked, too." Grasping one of the long axes that framed his throne, he lifted it high above his head and ran at Sir Balin, chopping down. Sir Balin parried the blow with his sword, but the axe cut right through the blade, leaving Sir Balin holding only a hilt.

King Perleus raised the axe again, and Lady Annalise shouted, "Run!"

Sir Balin turned and ran, with King Perleus at

his heels, chopping down every few steps with the axe. Sir Balin ran out of the high chamber, then turned right down a long corridor, then left at the next corridor, staying just ahead of King Perleus's blows. At last, Sir Balin realized he was coming to a dead end, a corridor that stopped at a door. He just managed to jump inside and slam the door behind him before King Perleus's axe smashed it open again. Sir Balin looked around

quickly and saw a long spear hanging on a hook over a fireplace. He took the spear down, whirled around, and threw it at King Perleus just as he entered the room.

King Perleus staggered and dropped his axe, Sir Balin's spear in his breast. "No! This can't happen!"

Sir Balin said nothing.

"You've killed me!"

"I was certainly trying to," panted Sir Balin.

"But I *can't* be killed!" King Perleus gasped. "The prophetess who attended my coronation said that I could not die until I ruled two kingdoms! I only rule one right now."

"Bad luck," Sir Balin said unsympathetically. "Prophecies can be a real pain, can't they?"

"And now both my kingdoms are gone! Indeed, Sir Balin, you have struck a dolorous stroke this day!"

Sir Balin blinked. "What did you say?"

"Look, I'm dying here, and you can't even be bothered to pay attention?" snapped King Perleus.

"Never mind," Sir Balin said. "I'm not interested anyway."

"But the prophecy said . . ."

"Prophecies say a lot of things," Sir Balin muttered. He closed the door behind him as he left the room.

Chapter 5
The Dolorous Death
of Sir Balin and Sir Balan

Once again, Sir Balin and Lady Annalise were
without a quest, but they agreed that until one
came along, they might as well ride together.
They decided they were as likely to find one together as separate, and whether that was true or
not, it worked for them.

"I thought you were about to give everything

away," Lady Annalise commented, "when you almost introduced yourself as the Knight with Two Swords."

"Yes, that was a near miss," Sir Balin agreed.

"Are you really from Northumberland? Because I'm from the north myself, from Carlisle."

Sir Balin peeked at her from the corner of his eye. "Fancy that," he said, thoughtfully.

"So what happened with King Perleus?"

"He missed me," Sir Balin said. "And I didn't miss him. Poor chap. He thought he was invincible."

"Why would he think that?"

"Because some meddling old prophetess at his coronation told him that he wouldn't die until he ruled two kingdoms. Apparently, that prophetess was full of bunk."

Lady Annalise nodded slowly. "Well, since you mention it, I *have* heard that the Prophetesses Guild has lowered its standards recently."

"There's a Prophetesses Guild?"

"There's a guild for everything. Somebody has to ensure quality work, don't you think?"

"I suppose I'd never thought about it," Sir Balin admitted. "But I am now. So, what if my brother Lannie is right? What if the prophetess at my christening was just spouting a bunch of rot?"

"I guess the only way to find out would be to test it. Why don't you try going against the prophecy and see if you can change your fate? What else did the Old Woman of the Mountain say?"

Sir Balin thought about this for a moment, then said, "Well, she prophesied that I would never turn down an adventure."

"And have you ever turned down an adventure?"

"Not yet," Sir Balin admitted. "But it's worth a go, don't you think?"

"I suppose," Lady Annalise said dubiously. "It's going to make it harder to find a quest, though."

"Nonsense," Sir Balin said. "It's the quest to defeat fate itself."

Lady Annalise smiled. "Brilliant! Why, that has to be the noblest quest of all!" She began to giggle. "Which, of course, makes you the noblest knight in England."

"Bother," said Sir Balin. "Not fulfilling my destiny may be harder than I thought."

As it happened, though, they had a chance to test their plan just a short time later. Riding through a gloomy forest, they came to a fork in the road. A sign pointed down the path that led to their right. The sign said, THIS WAY TO THE ADVENTURE OF THE ISLE OF BATTLES.

Sir Balin and Lady Annalise exchanged looks, then chose the left-hand path. "That wasn't so hard," Sir Balin commented.

Soon they came to another crossroad. A sign pointed to the left, saying, THE ADVENTURE OF THE ISLE OF BATTLES. They turned right. A few minutes later, they came to a third sign, pointing right. This one read, THIS WAY TO GLORY AND HONOR. They turned left again.

"Really, I could get used to this," Sir Balin said. "I never knew that avoiding adventure could be so enjoyable."

At that moment they emerged from the woods and found themselves in a small village beside a river. In the middle of the river was a long, treeless island with a small hut on one end. A narrow plank bridge led from the town to the island. As soon as they appeared, a throng of villagers

burst from their houses and ran to greet them. "At last! At last! A knight to save us!"

"What's all this?" Sir Balin asked.

A man with an official-looking sash pushed through the crowd, which parted for him. "O knight, I am the Lord Mayor of this town. We are cruelly oppressed by the Villainous Knight of the Isle of Battles! Save us! Save us! Before he destroys us all!"

Sir Balin frowned. "Is that the Isle of Battles?" he asked. "But the sign on the road said that it was the other direction."

The official looked about angrily until he saw a youth with red hair. "You! Clem! Didn't I tell you where to place those signposts?"

"Ay, your honor," replied Clem. "You said to make them point right-left-right, and I did." Clem scratched his head. "Did you mean right-left-right when you're facing *toward* the town or *away* from the—"

"You dunderhead!" roared the Lord Mayor. "No wonder nobody's been by in over a week! You pointed the signs the wrong way. Luckily, this knight found the right path anyway. It must have been fate! Will you save us, O knight, from the cruel Knight of the Island?"

Sir Balin sighed and looked at Lady Annalise. "Bother," he said. "It's one thing to turn down an adventure when nobody is hurt. It's another to turn away from people in need." Lady Annalise nodded, and Sir Balin said, "All right. I'll fight your villain."

"Excellent!" shouted the official. "We'll send word to the Knight of the Island that you're coming." One man ran across the plank bridge, while the rest of the townspeople lined up on the shore across from the island.

"I say," Sir Balin said, "I don't suppose you have a shield handy, do you?" Now that he was down to one sword and had a free hand, it occurred to him that a shield might be useful.

"Yes, of course," said the mayor. He led Sir Balin into a small structure nearby that was filled with shields. "Choose whichever you like."

"What are you doing with all these?" Sir Balin asked.

"They're, ah, sort of a town collection. A hobby, you might say."

Sir Balin chose a shield, then went to face the Knight of the Island. The bridge was too narrow for a horse, so he crossed to the island on foot. From the small hut at the other end, a knight in armor appeared. They looked at each other, then strode forward to fight.

Lady Annalise, watching with the villagers on the opposite shore, had seen many battles, but never had she seen such brilliant swordsmanship. Both knights nearly killed each other several times, but saved themselves by extraordinary skill. The crowd on the shore cheered loudly and appreciatively, but Lady Annalise felt no desire to join them. She was too worried for Sir Balin.

"This is our best one yet," said a townsman near her. "I'll wager a shilling on the Knight of the Island."

"You're on!" cried another. "What fun!"

Lady Annalise turned to stare at the villagers. Half were cheering for Sir Balin, but the other half were cheering for the Knight of the Island. All looked to be having a grand time.

On the island, the two knights separated and walked in a circle for a moment, evidently catching their breath. Lady Annalise looked again at the villagers. "This is all a big game to you, isn't it?" she demanded.

"Ay, my lady," replied a man nearby. "We wait for two knights to come by, tell the first one that we're about to be attacked by a villain, tell the second one that we're being oppressed by a villain, and then we get to watch them fight. It's as good as a tournament, but it's right here at home."

"But that's terrible!" Lady Annalise exclaimed. "A knight could get killed for your silly game!"

The townsman looked sulky. "They usually just get wounded," he muttered, "and we always give decent burials to the ones who die."

Lady Annalise started toward the bridge. "Balin! Wait!"

But it was too late. As she headed toward the island, the two battling knights struck at exactly the same moment, thrusting their swords into each other's hearts. Then, as one, they crumpled to the ground.

"Get back, all of you!" Lady Annalise shouted fiercely, shoving townspeople aside as she hurried toward the bridge. Alone, she raced across to the island, where she knelt over the two bodies. After several minutes, she rose to her feet and walked back to the bridge, glaring at the villagers.

"Do you want to hear what your cruel lies have done?" she said. Her voice was low, but it carried easily. "You think this is just a harmless game, but today you have slain two of the finest men in the land. There, behind me, lies Sir Balin, the Knight with Two Swords, and beside him in death lies his brother, Sir Balan the Doughty."

"His brother?" someone in the crowd muttered.

"Yes, his brother!" said Lady Annalise. "He did not recognize him because of his strange shield and because he had lost one of his two swords." She raised her eyes to heaven, and with a broken voice continued, "Alas, my friend Sir Balin! You tried to defy fate, but your fate caught up with you! It was foretold that you would destroy the knight whom you loved most in the world. Today that most tragic and dolorous fate has come upon you. Rest in peace, my friend! I and I alone shall carry you and your valorous brother back home to Northumberland!"

Shame on their faces, the villagers went to bring stretchers. They laid the two dead knights on them, then tied them behind their two horses. Her jaw clenched tightly, her shoulders shaking with suppressed emotion, Lady Annalise watched these preparations. Then she made the townspeople swear never to deceive good knights with their game again, and gave a few other instructions. When all had been done, she wordlessly mounted her own horse and led the knights' horses back into the woods, one hand covering her face, a picture of grief.

Epilogue

Two knights and a lady rode side by side on the Great North Road.

"What I don't understand," the lady was saying, "is how you recognized each other."

"We didn't at first," said one of the knights, who was, in fact, Sir Balin. "Lannie was wearing a new suit of armor from the town's collection, and as you said, I was carrying a shield and was down to only one sword."

"But it didn't take long," interposed the other knight, Sir Balan. "You see, Lin and I have sparred with each other since we were old enough to hold wooden swords. We know all each other's tricks and weaknesses."

"Mostly weaknesses in Lannie's case," added Sir Balin.

"Put a cork in it," said Sir Balan.

"So," continued Sir Balin, "once we had figured out who the other was, we separated and walked in a circle, comparing each other's stories. When we figured out that we had just been set up to fight for the town's entertainment, we decided to give them a show and kill each other. It isn't that hard to fake if you do it right."

"But I must say, Lady Annalise," Sir Balan added, "it wouldn't have worked nearly so well without your help. That was an inspired speech. I almost cried."

"He always cries after we fight," Sir Balin said.

"How many times do I have to tell you," Sir Balan said wearily. *"Put a cork in it!* I especially like the way you made the villagers burn the bridge to the island after we'd been carried off."

"I wasn't sure they would keep their promise," Lady Annalise said. "I'm still not sure of that, but at least it will be harder for them for a bit."

"All in all," Sir Balan said, "I think it was a lucky day when Lin met you. But he's always been a lucky chap."

"I quite agree," replied Lady Annalise, nodding. "He's been a Questing Lady's dream, and he's brought me excellent fortune."

Sir Balin blinked, then smiled slowly. "You know what? You're right. I've had a very lucky life."

Two days later, they arrived at the brothers' home in Northumberland. Their parents, grayer but otherwise looking just as they had twenty years before, greeted them with delight and welcomed Lady Annalise with open arms.

They had a splendid dinner, then retired together to the same firelit parlor where the Old Woman of an Indeterminate Mountain had made her prophecies so long ago. There, Sir Balin told the story of his quests. When he was done, his father pursed his lips thoughtfully.

"So, in the end," he said, "was that old woman right or not? You did become known as the noblest knight in England."

"Yes," said Sir Balin, "but I wasn't. It was just that I accidentally muddled up a lie cooked up by two traitors."

"Accidentally. Yes, of course," said his father. "And you did strike the Dolorous Stroke."

"King Perleus *did* use that word," Sir Balin admitted. "But I'm nearly certain that he said *a* dolorous stroke."

"He said *dolorous*?" murmured Sir Balan. "I mean, really, who says *dolorous*?"

Their father continued, "And by striking that *dolorous* stroke, you brought down two kingdoms."

"But they weren't real kingdoms," Sir Balin argued. "At least one was only imaginary. It only existed in King Perleus's own head, placed there by another silly prophetess."

"The Old Woman of the Mountain never said they had to be *real* kingdoms," replied his father. "Moreover, you never turned down an adventure."

"Yes, I did!" Sir Balin exclaimed. "Three times!"

"No, you didn't," replied his father, "you tried to, but you ended up taking it after all."

At this point, his wife interrupted. "Dear, please be quiet. The old woman's prophecy is nonsense and always was. Balin didn't destroy the knight he loves most in the world, because his brother's right here. Most of all, he hasn't brought misfortune on everyone he meets. He saved King Arthur from two traitors and from the rebel King Royns, he got rid of that horrid invisible knight and his equally horrid brother, and he put a stop to that nasty custom at the Isle of Battles. So, really, Balin's always bringing *good* fortune."

"My dear," said her husband indulgently, "you would say that even if—"

"I *said*, Balin's always bringing good fortune."

"Yes, dear."

At this, Sir Balin spoke. "I think I'm with Mother here. Things only went bad for me when I was trying to live according to the prophecy. Once I started to doubt it and to make my own way, things worked out much better for me. I'm through with prophecies now."

Sir Balin's mother smiled at him and said, "In the end, there's really only one prophecy that matters, and I can see that one will come true very soon."

Sir Balin looked confused. "I thought we'd agreed the prophecy was just silly."

"Not the old woman's prophecy. Mine! Haven't I always predicted that you'd marry a nice northern girl?"

Sir Balin and Lady Annalise glanced furtively at each other. Sir Balin cleared his throat. "What do you say, Annalise?"

Lady Annalise shrugged. "What can I say? It's fate."

"A prophecy's a prophecy," Sir Balin said, nodding soberly.

"I guess we'll just have to accept it," said Lady Annalise, smiling.

Sir Balan rolled his eyes. "Oh, put a cork in it, both of you," he said.

Many years ago, the storytellers say, the great King Arthur brought justice to England with the help of his gallant Knights of the Round Table. Behold, dear reader, more hilarious and high-spirited adventures from The Knights' Tales, as only the acclaimed Arthurian author Gerald Morris can tell them!

Sir Lancelot the Great

Never was one so fearless, so chivalrous, so honorable, so . . . *shiny* as the dashing Sir Lancelot, who was quite good at defending the helpless and protecting the weak, just as long as he'd had his afternoon nap.

★"Rejoice, fans of the Squire's Tales . . . Morris is finally bringing his terrific recastings of Arthurian legend to a younger audience. . . . More, please." —*Kirkus Reviews*, starred review

"The art catches the tone of the writing in the often-amusing ink drawings. A promising series debut for young readers." —*Booklist*

"The book's brevity and humor make it accessible to reluctant readers, and it is a fantastic read-aloud." —*School Library Journal*

"This trim novel, with simple vocabulary and brief, witty chapters, is an ideal fit for early readers . . . but fans of the legendary characters may find particular delight in this irreverent and unabashedly silly exploration of Arthur's court and his most influential knight." —*The Bulletin*

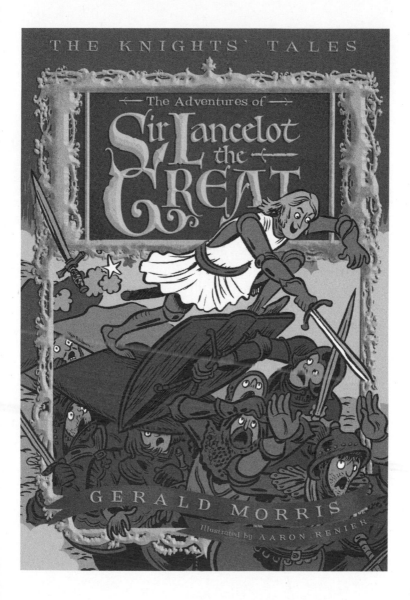

Sir Givret the Short

Poor Givret—since he's easily the shortest man at court, his size makes him easy to overlook. But what he lacks in stature Givret makes up for with clever thinking. Surely there's more to knighthood than height! So beginneth the adventures of Sir Givret the Short, the Brilliant, and the Marvelous.

> "Delivers more quests and adventures geared for a younger audience than the author's Squire's Tales books. . . . Brush and ink illustrations, both full-page and vignettes, are scattered throughout, adding interest to the humorous story line . . . a reckless young knight out to prove himself results in an entertaining tale that is sure to please young readers."
> —*School Library Journal*

> "The books in Morris's Knights' Tales series feature short, episodic chapters and funny little illustrations of knightly derring-do . . . the emphasis is on cleverness over heroism. . . . This is often quite funny, and just exciting enough to capture the attention of budding young Arthur-philes." —*Booklist*

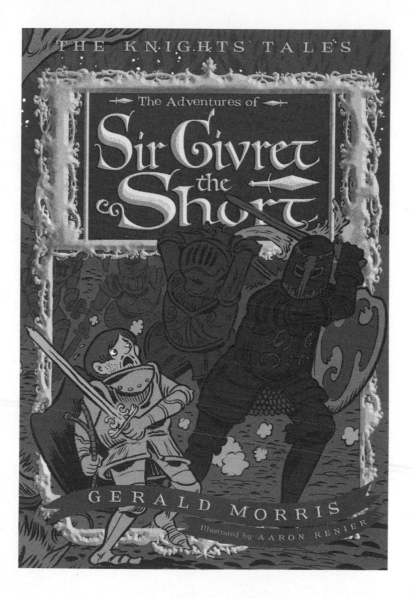

THE KNIGHTS' TALES

The Adventures of

Sir Givret the Short

GERALD MORRIS

Illustrated by AARON RENIER

Sir Gawain the True

Hear ye, hear ye! Joust into the laugh-out-loud tale of King Arthur's most celebrated knight, and nephew, Sir Gawain, who is more skilled at winning tournaments than making friends. Can it be that courtesy is as important as courage?

"Broad humor graced with lively language will have readers laughing along with this boisterous Arthurian adventure." — *Yellow Brick Road*

★ "An ingeniously integrated retelling of Gawain and the Green Knight and other episodes from the Arthurian canon. Worthy reading for all budding squires and damsels."
— *Kirkus Reviews,* starred review

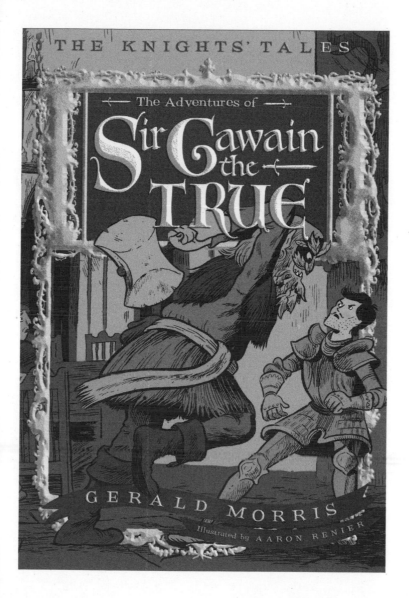

THE KNIGHTS' TALES

The Adventures of

Sir Gawain the TRUE

GERALD MORRIS

Illustrated by AARON RENIER